For all the Children & Moms who need this book, & for all who will simply fall in love with it. This is for you ♥

Dedicated To:
My beautiful daughter Perri Rain, &
my beautiful mother Vickie

To My Boys:
Zachary, Nicholas & Vincent ... You
are forever in my heart

For My Dad:
Thank You for always helping & believing in me

To My Friends, Family, & SNUUC Family...
Thank You for being in my life. I love you all

Balboa Press books may be ordered through booksellers or by contacting:

Balboa Press
A Division of Hay House
1663 Liberty Drive
Bloomington, IN 47403
www.balboapress.com
1 (877) 407–4847

Original Illustrations by: Patricia Grace
Recreated by: Toni Germie

ISBN: 978–1–9822–3924–4 (sc)
ISBN: 978–1–9822–3925–1 (e)

Print information available on the last page.

Balboa Press rev. date: 12/06/2019

Hi, my name is Randy Rabbit.
My Mommy's name is Kelly Kangaroo.
We don't look alike, but
I know she is my Mommy
And I'll tell you how I know it's true.

I know she is my Mommy because
she teaches me my A B C's.

I know she is my Mommy because
she has tissues when I sneeze.

I know she is my Mommy because
she helps me tie my shoe.

I know she is my Mommy because
she cheers me when I'm blue.

I know she is my Mommy because
she checks for the "Boogie Man"
under my bed.

I know she is my Mommy because I'm
neatly dressed and **always fed.**

I know she is my Mommy because
she has band-aids for my knee.

I know she is my Mommy because
when I cry **she comforts** me.

I know she is my Mommy because
she tells me stories before bed.

I know she is my Mommy because
she knows the thoughts running through my head.

Put all these things together

and pretty soon you'll see…

That I know she is my Mommy because
she *shows* her **love** for me.

About the Author:

Lisa Itts was born in Brooklyn, New York but at 6 months of age moved to Hazlet, New Jersey and spent her formative years there. At 8, she moved to Long Island, New York and started on her musical journey. She began learning guitar at age 9 and started to write songs by age 11. She picked up learning the piano in college, majored in early childhood education and minored in music . She went on to teach guitar, piano, and voice, and write and perform music professionally. Lisa has been recognized internationally for her songwriting and has performed nationally.

Lisa always loved writing and at age 24 she had the opportunity to write a children's book as a project for an English class in college. This is where "I Know She Is My Mommy" ... was born. Lisa felt there was a need in society for a children's book about how a child knows and/or connects and bonds with their mother, weather biological, adopted, coming from same–sex parents, interracial etc.

During the coming years, Lisa tried to publish this book, but it seemed Society wasn't ready. Now her dream of being published by Balboa press & Hay House has come true.

More recently, Lisa has continued with her passion for music, writing, and helping, by attending nursing school and also starting to write and record music again after a sabbatical in order to raise her children.

"Be good to people. You will be remembered
more for your kindness than any level of success
you could possibly attain." ~ Mandy Hale

Message from the Author:

I felt there was a need in society for a children's book about how a child knows and/or connects and bonds with their mother, weather biological, adopted, coming from same—sex parents, interracial etc. Although I wrote this Book almost 20 years ago, I feel its true timing is now, and my dream of being published by Balboa press & Hay House has finally come to fruition.

"To everything there is a season, and a time
for every purpose under the heaven"
Ecclesiastes 3:1—8, KJV

Contact Info:
Website: www.lisaitts.com
Facebook: lisaitts
YouTube: Lisa Itts

Printed in the United States
By Bookmasters